ISBN 0-86163-735-6

Copyright © 1994 Award Publications Limited

First published 1994 by Award Publications Limited
Goodyear House, 52–56 Osnaburgh Street,
London, NW1 3NS

Printed in Spain

LINDA JENNINGS

WITCHES GALORE
and other Magical Stories

Illustrated by

VAL BIRO

AWARD PUBLICATIONS LIMITED

CONTENTS

The Witch's New Broomstick   8

The Last Wizard   12

The Lost Rabbit   15

Felicity Witch   18

The Daisy Ring   22

Playing Wizards   25

The Witch Trap   29

The Travelling Witch   33

The Spelling Book   37

Fairy Cakes   40

The Hallowe'en Party   43

The New Broom   47

Nat's Magic Seedling   51

The Broomstick Race   53

The Magic Bicycle   56

The Monster Under the Pavement   59

The Magic Stone   63

Cat on a Broomstick   66

Dragon Fire   69

The Little Yellow Goblin   73

The Monster in the Pool   76

All That Glitters . . .   80

Not Quite a Dragon   83

Witch Twinkletoes   87

The Witch at the Bottom of the Lane   90

THE WITCH'S NEW BROOMSTICK

Witch Nightshade had broken her broomstick. The twigs had come apart one night as she was flying over Hightop Wood. Luckily for her, she had managed to land in the branches of a tree and so break her fall.

But how could she fly anywhere without a broomstick?

"I must go into town and buy a new one," she decided.

Witch Nightshade marched into a shop.

"A broomstick?" asked the shop assistant, looking down his nose at Witch Nightshade. She was not the tidiest of witches. Her cloak needed mending and her stockings had holes in them.

"I'm afraid there's not much demand for old-fashioned broomsticks nowadays."

"But there is – I am demanding one," retorted Witch Nightshade.

"I'm afraid I can't order in a complete new stock, just for one – um – old – er – person," said the shop assistant.

"Well, what *can* I do?" wailed Witch Nightshade. "I can't go anywhere without my broom. What do people buy instead of broomsticks, then?"

"Vacuum cleaners," replied the shop assistant.

"I don't think I've ever seen one of those," said Witch Nightshade. "Perhaps I'd better take a look."

The man looked doubtfully at Witch Nightshade. She didn't look as though she had two pennies to rub together, let alone enough money to buy a vacuum cleaner. Reluctantly he led the witch through the shop into the showroom beyond.

"Ooh," breathed Witch Nightshade. "What *lovely* machines." She went over to a streamlined green and beige vacuum cleaner and lovingly stroked it. "I would be a sensation at the coven with one of these," she said to herself. "I really *must* buy one."

"That will be eighty-one pounds and sixty-five pence," said the shop assistant as Witch Nightshade started pushing the cleaner round the floor. "And I'm afraid we don't take credit cards."

"That's all right," said Witch Nightshade. "I can pay cash."

She took out a large, well-worn purse and began pulling five-pound notes from it. The shop assistant could have sworn the purse was empty when she'd first opened it. He took the notes and held them up to the light.

"Just to be sure they're genuine," he told her with a smile. Then he pocketed the money and took a large cardboard box from behind the counter.

"No need to pack it," said Witch Nightshade. "I'll ride it home."

"Ride it!" exclaimed the shop assistant.

"Of course, it's not quite what I'm used to, but I expect I'll soon learn," said the witch, and to the young man's astonishment she zoomed right out of the shop and slowly took to the air – slowly because the vacuum cleaner was far heavier than a broomstick. All the same, within seconds she had vanished from the amazed assistant's sight.

Witch Nightshade was absolutely right. She was a sensation at the local coven!

The shop assistant was even more amazed when he was visited by a large crowd of very strangely dressed ladies, each demanding a vacuum cleaner. Within a couple of days he had sold right out of them.

So, if you ever go out at midnight on Hallowe'en, you may hear a very strange sound – a whole army of vacuum cleaners passing overhead!

THE LAST WIZARD

Did you know that the last really
magical wizard left in England
was a little boy called Mervyn?
Mervyn was, as all wizards are,
the seventh son of a seventh son.
That's very rare nowadays, because
people don't have such big families,
and no one believes in magic anyway.
So when Mervyn was born, wizards
were really rather thin on the ground.
Come to think of it, have *you* ever seen a real wizard dressed in
long black robes and a tall hat with stars on? I bet you haven't.

At first Mervyn was delighted to learn that he was a wizard.
It made him very popular at school because he could cast spells to
make everyone's maths homework correct and, in the school
football match, he'd see to it that his team always scored the
winning goal.

But, as time went on, Mervyn grew rather tired of casting spells to suit all his friends. In fact, being a wizard was a positive embarrassment. Like most children, he didn't like to be different. He didn't want to be pointed out as the school wizard because he was always being asked to prove it by casting a spell.

"I don't want to be a wizard any more, Mum," Mervyn complained one day at dinner.

"Well, you'll just have to put up with it," said Mum. "Once a wizard, always a wizard. You ought to be pleased. You're the only wizard left in England – and Europe, too, I expect."

But Mervyn pushed his sausages round the plate and sulked. He was so fed up that he couldn't even be bothered to change the sausages into miniature dachshunds.

"I don't know what to do," Mervyn complained to his friend, Darren. "I've got this great big spellbook that belonged to my great-great grandfather. Somehow I can't help casting spells from it, however much I don't want to."

Darren thought hard. "Suppose I borrow it from you," he said. "And then sort of lose it?"

"Dad would be furious," said Mervyn. "And what do you mean, lose it? It mustn't get into the wrong hands."

"Leave it to me," said Darren, so Mervyn did. The next day he lent Darren the book and the following day it had conveniently disappeared. Mervyn was quite unable to cast any spells at all.

His dad roared and raved, but nothing could be done.

But what had happened to the spellbook?

Thousands of miles away, 'down under' in Australia, Darren's aunt was celebrating her birthday. Eagerly, she undid the parcel from her nephew, and cackled with delight.

"Ah, at last! The very thing I've been looking for for years!" she exclaimed. She couldn't wait to begin! For Darren's Australian aunt was the seventh daughter of a seventh daughter!

14

THE LOST RABBIT

On the day of Simon's birthday party his pet rabbit, Thumper, disappeared. Simon found the hutch door open. He felt dreadful because he realised he had forgotten to do up the latch the night before. Thumper was a beautiful white angora rabbit, and Simon was sure that he must have been stolen.

Poor Simon! How could he look forward to his party, or to the special surprise Mum and Dad had laid on for him? He was far too worried about Thumper.

When his friends arrived, one by one, all Simon could manage was the most watery of smiles. To make it worse, one of his friends, Carla, had brought him a special brush for Thumper.

"Thank you," he said in a very small voice.

Simon cheered up a little bit when they went in to tea and he blew out seven red candles on his train-shaped birthday cake. He cheered up even more when Mum led the children into the living room and sat them in rows on the floor.

"Now for the surprise," said Mum.

A very strange man, dressed in a long royal blue robe with silver stars on it, swept into the room. He had a tall black hat on his head.

It was a conjuror!

"Magician," corrected the man, as one of Simon's friends asked him if he was the same conjuror his mum had booked for his own party the following week.

"I only visit an area once," said the magician, mysteriously. "Too much strong magic in the atmosphere is very bad – it's rather like electric shocks."

He waved his wand and the children gasped in surprise. The back wall of the room, which was covered with flowered wallpaper, suddenly became a real garden with the wallpaper flowers blowing gently in the breeze!

Even Nick, who said he knew how every trick was done, was dumbstruck.

A wonderful display of magic followed. The magician waved his wand at the television and the people on the screen walked right out of the set! Luckily it was a ballet scene. A gangster film might have been more tricky! Soon the ballet dancers disappeared, giving way to an amazing firework display. Finally the magician produced a shiny black top hat.

"And what would you like me to produce for you out of this hat?" he asked the children.

Everyone shouted at once, but the magician turned to Simon.

"You're the birthday boy," he said. "You choose – but don't tell anyone what it is."

Simon shut his eyes tightly, and wished and wished . . .

The magician waved his wand once, twice, three times. And out of his hat he produced – you've guessed, of course – one fluffy white angora rabbit!

"Thumper!" shouted Simon, jumping up. And Thumper it was. Simon knew him at once for he had a black spot under his chin. But had the magician stolen him? Simon didn't think so. After all, the magic he had used hadn't been the usual conjuror sort of magic. It had been real!

No, somehow Simon's wishes and the magician's magic had brought Thumper right back home from wherever he had been.

It was Simon's best birthday present ever!

FELICITY WITCH

In an old cottage, right on the edge of a dark wood, there lived a witch. She had a hunched back, a huge wart on her nose, and long fingers like gnarled twigs. She wore a floppy old hat and she was called Felicity.

She also had a cat called Midnight.

One day Felicity Witch received a letter from Chief Witch Hemlock.

You are summonsed to appear before the coven next Friday, 13th May, at midnight prompt. DO NOT BE LATE!

Felicity Witch trembled. It sounded most alarming! What could be wrong? As far as she knew she was a good witch. She cast all the right spells and she never missed a coven. True, she had rather more visitors than was usual for a witch for besides her spells she did make the most delicious blackcurrant tea!

She always held a tea-party every Tuesday afternoon for all the ladies in the village. They all seemed to like her tea, and they even liked Felicity Witch who wasn't nearly so alarming as she looked, once you got to know her.

Felicity Witch arrived early at the coven. As her sister witches flew down on their broomsticks, Felicity Witch gave them her usual smile and they smiled back. It was quite a cheerful gathering. Felicity Witch began to feel better.
Perhaps the summons wasn't going to be so dreadful after all.
Then Chief Witch Hemlock flew down on her broomstick. She was a tall and rather bad-tempered witch. She saw all the witches talking cheerfully together and landed in the middle of the gathering.

"THIS IS ALL FELICITY WITCH'S DOING!" she roared.
"What?" asked Felicity innocently.

"All this laughing and carrying on. It's because of your smile.
It warms people's hearts. It makes them cheerful, it makes
friends of enemies," said Chief Witch Hemlock.

"I don't have any enemies," said Felicity Witch, giving Chief
Witch Hemlock one of her warmest and most dazzling smiles.

"THERE YOU GO AGAIN – STOP IT!" roared Chief Witch
Hemlock.

"I can't," said poor Felicity. "It's part of me. Perhaps it's
because my mother called me Felicity. It means 'happiness'."

"Then we'll just change your name," said Chief Witch
Hemlock. "We'll call you Griselda or Haggerty or Wartsnap!"

Felicity stopped smiling. "I don't like any of those names,
they're ugly."

"I ORDER you to be called Wartsnap," said Chief Witch
Hemlock. "And I'm Chief Witch, so there!"

Poor Felicity flew home again. She felt very miserable with her new name and didn't smile once. On Tuesday afternoon, her friends came round for their blackcurrant tea and they saw an old and unhappy witch, as ugly as sin. But they weren't frightened. They knew Felicity too well. They put their arms round her and hugged her.

"Cheer up," they said. "Give us one of your lovely smiles." Felicity managed a very watery one.

"That's better. Now put your feet up, and we'll make *you* a cup of tea."

Felicity/Wartsnap looked round at all her friends' concerned faces.

"What's in a name?" she thought. "It's who you are that matters."

And she beamed round at all her Tuesday afternoon ladies with one of her most dazzling and beautiful smiles.

THE DAISY RING

Mr Trimble was a very neat man. He had a neat, trim garden with wonderful displays of flowers and not a weed or bug in sight. But his pride and joy was his lawn – a deep, rich green velvet.

One day Mr Trimble looked out of his bedroom window and he gave a loud bellow of rage.

What was that in the middle of his lovely velvety lawn?

It was a ring of white daisies.

Mr Trimble rushed downstairs and into his garden shed. He pulled out his lawnmower and ran it across the lawn until all the daisy heads were chopped off. Then he took his weedkiller and sprinkled it on the headless daisy plants.

"That'll fix 'em," he growled but, to his horror, the very next morning the daisy ring was back!

Over the next few weeks Mr Trimble tried in vain to rid himself of the troublesome daisy ring, but without success. Every morning when he looked out of his window he saw a new ring of daisies. It seemed to him, too, that the daisies were growing bigger and stronger.

Mr Trimble made a decision. It would be better to have no lawn at all than a lawn full of untidy daisies. He arranged for it to be covered in black tarmac.

"I can always put pots of plants on it," he said to himself.

That night, Mr Trimble was woken by a strange sound. It sounded like someone chipping at stone. He rushed to the window, and what do you think he saw?

A group of tiny people were in the middle of the tarmac, attacking it with pickaxes.

"HOW DARE THEY!" roared Mr Trimble. He pulled on his dressing-gown and ran out into the garden, without even putting his slippers on.

"What do you think you're doing?" he cried. "You're ruining my garden!"

A tiny little fellow, no bigger than Mr Trimble's foot, stood with his arms folded, looking very cross indeed.

"Ruining your garden! That's exactly what you're doing, you stupid man! Our poor little daisy ring can't push through all that ugly black tarmac."

"Good job, too," growled Mr Trimble.

The little man danced with rage. "There's gratitude for you!" he screeched. "Who do you think makes your plants grow so well? Why don't you ever get any caterpillars or bugs?"

"I – I don't know," stuttered Mr Trimble.

"It's us, you stupid great human. We do it. But unless there's a fairy ring, we can't come."

Mr Trimble gave a big sigh. If he insisted on destroying the fairy ring he'd have no prize blooms. If he didn't, he'd have an untidy lawn. It was a difficult choice, but he did love his flowers.

"All right," he said. "I'll get rid of the tarmac."

In time Mr Trimble even grew to love the daisy ring. It was really quite pretty in the middle of his green velvet lawn.

PLAYING WIZARDS

Harry's uncle was a wizard. He could cast spells on people, and even turn old bottle tops into tenpenny pieces. This made Harry very popular at school, because everyone thought that wizardry must run in the family and that Harry must be able to do a spell or two.

"Oh, go on," pleaded Sam. "Just one little spell."

"*I'm* not a wizard," said Harry. "I can't do any magic."

"I bet you could if you tried," said Sam. "If you watch what your uncle does, or steal his spellbook, I bet you could cast a spell."

Sam went on and on about it, until finally Harry began to think that perhaps he *could* do some magic if he tried. He didn't like the idea of stealing the spellbook, but the very next time he visited his uncle he asked him if he could turn Buttercup the canary into a vulture, and then back again.

Harry watched carefully as his uncle mixed this and that. He took note of all the ingredients, and he listened to the magic words his uncle muttered as he smeared the mixture all over the canary's feathers.

Buttercup began to sprout a cruel-looking beak, and she grew to ten times her size!

Harry watched just as carefully as his uncle changed the vulture back into Buttercup again.

The next day, Harry and Sam met in Harry's den at the bottom of the garden. Sam had brought his hamster with him because neither boy had a canary.

"I expect it will work just as well," said Harry confidently. He looked at the piece of paper where he had secretly scribbled down the ingredients for the spell:

Three teaspoonsful of chopped ivyleaf.

A dash of toad's spittle.

Seven deadly nightshade berries.

A mouse's paw.

The second and the last items proved rather difficult to find, but at last Sam found a toad in the rockery. When he picked it up and dangled it over the spell-bowl, it spat out a spurt of liquid. Harry's cat had brought in a mouse that morning and had eaten it all but for the tail.

"I expect that will do instead," said Harry.

The mixture looked disgusting. Harry stirred it three times in one direction and three times in the other, muttering the words he'd heard his uncle use. Then he began to dab the mixture over the hamster's fur.

The spell began to work. The hamster grew larger and larger.

"I can't see any sign of a beak," remarked Sam, backing nervously away from his giant pet.

"It's not changing into a vulture!" gasped Harry. "It's a much bigger animal. Help, I think it's going to be an elephant!"

Sure enough, the hamster's neat little nose began to grow longer and longer, and his ears larger and larger. The boys found that the shed was too small to take them all, and they opened the door and backed out.

That was a mistake. Before Harry had time to reverse the spell, the elephant put its huge foot on the bowl of mixture and broke it to pieces. All the mixture was pounded into the ground. Then the elephant gave an enormous trumpeting cry and stampeded out of the shed, right across Dad's row of cabbages, and out through the open gate.

"Stop him!" yelled Harry. He tried to scoop up some of the spilt mixture in his hands, but by the time the two boys reached the gate the elephant was out of sight.

I can't imagine what might have happened next, but luckily Harry's uncle always put a safety element into his spells in case they got into the wrong hands. So he wasn't at all surprised when the elephant arrived at his front door and rapped the knocker with his trunk.

In a couple of stamps of an elephant's foot, Sam's hamster was restored to its former self. Harry's uncle telephoned Harry and asked him to collect it.

"Never mess around with spells," he told Harry firmly. "If you can't get a spell absolutely right, just don't try it at all."

Harry promised faithfully that he wouldn't.

THE WITCH TRAP

There was once a witch called Dreadnought. She was as nasty a witch as you would find anywhere, and she spent all her time adding more and more spells to her great leather-bound spellbook.

She could change dogs into centipedes.

She could turn a mouth-watering beef stew into a mess of mouldy, rotting vegetables that smelt of old socks.

She could transform a young bride on her wedding day into a bent old hag even uglier than herself.

"We have to do something about her," said Mayor Nettletwist, the day he found his ceremonial carriage changed into a rusty old wheelbarrow. "We must stop her from making all our lives a misery."

All the citizens of the town agreed. There was not one of them who had not suffered at least once from Witch Dreadnought's nasty spells. But what could they do?

The Mayor had a plan. They would burn the old witch's spellbook, and at the same time they would make her tremble and shake with fear.

Witch Dreadnought always walked across the fields to Chestnut Wood every Monday morning. She went there to collect dead flies, toadstools, and anything else she needed for her spells. She always took the same route.

One particular Monday, Witch Dreadnought was stomping across the fields. There was a sudden loud *crack!* and a *crash!* The witch disappeared into a big hole that had been hidden by branches and grass. She had left her spellbook at home so there was no spell she could weave to get herself out. The Mayor stood at the edge of the field and laughed.

"We'll have to break into her cottage to get the spellbook," he said. "Then we'll see some fun."

All the townsfolk hurried across the field to where the old witch was screeching and shouting fit to burst.

"Let me out!" she howled. "I'll change you all into mice and get my cat to eat you! I'll make warts grow all over your noses! I'll –"

"Oh no, you won't," said the Mayor. "We've got the spellbook. We're going to do all those things to you!"

And Mr Chop, the butcher, waved the spellbook across the top of the hole at her. He and Mr Stitch, the tailor, had broken down her door. They all knew that stealing was wrong, but making people's lives a misery was even worse.

The witch howled and yelled with rage, but there was nothing she could do. She doubted if the people could use the spellbook, anyway. They hadn't the training to work spells. But she still couldn't get out of the hole.

She sat crouched in the darkness. Everyone was out of sight, but she could hear them outside in the field. They were doing something . . . She could smell smoke!

Oh no! They were lighting a fire!

"What do we do to witches?" asked the Mayor.

"Burn them!" cried the people.

Witch Dreadnought began to shiver and shake. "No, no, you can't burn me – I'll turn you into – " But of course, she couldn't.

The Mayor poked his head over the top of the hole. "Are you ready for your punishment, Witch Dreadnought?" he asked.

Witch Dreadnought couldn't speak. She shivered and shook until her hat fell off.

"It's nice and hot," someone remarked.

31

"Aaaagh!" cried the witch, in panic.

"It's burning! It's burning!" cried someone else, and then Witch Dreadnought realised that it was her precious spellbook that was being consumed by the flames! They might come for her next!

"Will you promise never to make another spellbook?" asked the Mayor, suddenly feeling sorry for the old woman. Without her magic she was nothing but an old woman.

"No, of course not!" she cried. "A witch must have a spellbook."

"Very well then, but only with *good* spells," said the Mayor.

"What fun are good spells?" thought Witch Dreadnought. Then she smelt the burnt leather of her book and thought of what might happen if she didn't agree.

"Very well," she said. "A witch's promise."

The Mayor threw down a rope and helped her climb out of the hole.

Witch Dreadnought bought a new spellbook. From it she made potions, creams and spells for curing and healing and making the ugly beautiful. She even began to enjoy herself and make friends. After a while she was known as, not Witch Dreadnought, but the Good Witch Cureall.

THE TRAVELLING WITCH

Wanda Witch flung her cloak round her, rammed on her tall black hat, and calling to her cat, Blackberry, she went out into her backyard to collect her broomstick. She sat astride it and Blackberry crouched behind.

"To Humpty Bumpty Hill!" she ordered, but to her extreme annoyance the broomstick didn't move. It didn't even twitch so much as a twig. Wanda kicked it angrily.

"Get *going*!" she screeched, shaking the handle. "We'll be late for the coven."

But the broomstick stayed still. It was as though it was just an ordinary broomstick instead of a magic one. Wanda Witch thought very hard.

"The magic must have worn out," said Wanda. "I'll need a new spell to revive it. There's certainly no time for that now!"

Blackberry sat in the yard, washing himself carefully.

"What *shall* I do?" she wailed at Blackberry. "It's a very important meeting," she went on. "They're going to choose a new Chief Witch and it's said that I'm tipped for the job!"

"You could go by rail," suggested Blackberry.

Wanda wondered what people would say if they saw a witch boarding a train but she didn't really have much choice. The broomstick was well and truly unmagicked.

Wanda put Blackberry into his cat-basket and ran all the way down the lane to the railway station.

"What time's the next train to Humpty Bumpty Hill?" she asked the ticket collector.

"Never heard of it," said the man, staring hard at Wanda. "Are you going to some kind of fancy-dress party?"

"Of course not," snapped Wanda. "You must have heard of Humpty Bumpty Hill. It's famous!"

"For what?"

"Why, for covens, of course," she said angrily. "Everyone knows that!"

"Well, *I* don't," said the ticket collector. "I don't even know what a coven is."

Wanda could hear the sound of a train approaching.

"Hurry up!" she cried. "Humpty Bumpty Hill – " She snapped her bony fingers at him. "Quick, or I'll turn you into a toad."

"I know Humpty Bumpty Hill," came a voice from behind her. "Take the train to Chatterbox Junction, then walk down the lane and turn right. The hill is straight ahead of you."

Wanda barely thanked the lady who had given her the information. She grabbed her ticket and sped on to the platform.

"Don't forget me!" wailed Blackberry, for Wanda had left his basket in the ticket office. But she didn't hear him. She flung open the door of a carriage and leapt on, just as the train was beginning to move. A sudden gust of wind removed her tall hat and it went bowling away along the platform.

At Chatterbox Junction, Wanda Witch got out. She followed the lane, and very soon she saw Humpty Bumpty Hill ahead of her.

"Thank goodness, just in time," she gasped as she huffed and puffed up the steep hill to the top.

The coven was just beginning. Fifty witches were gathered there, each with her own black cat.

Wanda Witch arrived. She was hatless and catless and without her broomstick.

The Chief Witch stared hard at Wanda Witch.

"What have we here?" she asked. "An Outsider at our coven? Away with you – this meeting is for witches only."

"But I *am* a witch," said Wanda. "I'm Wanda Witch – you all know me. I was hoping to be your new leader."

"Wanda Witch – nonsense!" said the Chief Witch. "Wanda Witch, like every witch, has a broomstick, a black cat, and a tall hat. You have none of these things, therefore you can't be a witch."

Wanda tried to tell them all about her broomstick, about the train, and about poor Blackberry whom she had left behind at the station. But they wouldn't listen. They all got to their feet and shooed her away with their broomsticks. Wanda Witch fled.

She had a long wait at the station for the early morning train. And when she got back to her own station she found that Blackberry had been released from his basket. He was sitting comfortably on a station bench.

"I'm staying here," he said. "I'm fed up with being a witch's cat. I want to be a station cat instead."

Poor Wanda Witch returned to her cottage without her cat and without her hat. The Chief Witch had said she couldn't be a witch without these things. Well, perhaps she wouldn't be a witch any more. Perhaps she would join the Senior Citizens' Club and go on outings to Blackpool . . .

Wanda Witch felt a whole new life was just beginning . . .

THE SPELLING BOOK

Jenny found the book on a second-hand book stall. On the tatty red leather cover was written in black: *SPELLING BOOK*. She chose it because she couldn't spell very well.

As soon as she was home, Jenny opened the book. She expected to see lists of difficult words that she could learn by heart, but instead there were a lot of funny-looking squiggles and numbers. She was very disappointed. "What's the use of a spelling book if it's written in a foreign language and I can't read it?" she said.

Jenny threw the book to the back of her cupboard in disgust, and that might have been the end of that.

But it wasn't.

The following week, Jenny returned to the same book stall and began to browse through the books.

"I hope you have something I can read this time," she joked. "That spelling book I bought last week was useless."

The old woman behind the stall stared at her hard. "Did you say *spelling book*?" she asked. "Was it covered in red leather with big black lettering?"

Jenny nodded. "That's it," she said.

"Thank goodness for that," said the woman. "The book was thrown out by mistake. It belongs to Mr Merlin and he wants it back."

"He can have it," said Jenny. "It's no good to me."

"I'll tell you what," said the woman. "Would you be a dear and return the book yourself? You can choose anything you like from the stall – take two, to make up for the spelling book."

Jenny chose a pony book and an old Christmas annual, and the lady told her where the man, Mr Merlin, lived.

Directly after lunch, Jenny set off for Mr Merlin's house. Her mother came too, and waited for her at the gate. Jenny saw that the brass knocker was a funny-looking dragon. She could have sworn it winked at her! She felt a bit afraid as she knocked at the door.

The man who opened it was very tall and very thin. He had a long white beard and big bushy eyebrows. His eyes were a piercing, deep blue, and he stared hard at Jenny.

"I've brought your book back," she said. "The spelling book."

The old man clapped his hands and gave a big whoop of joy. "My spelling book!" he cried. "You've found it! I can't do my job without my spelling book."

Jenny was beginning to understand what the book really was. "It's for spells, isn't it?" she said.

The old man bowed gravely as he took the book from her hands. "I am Merlin the Wizard," he said. "Named after the greatest magician of all. But, my dear, you must have a reward. Come in."

Jenny asked if her mother could come too. No wise child would walk unaccompanied into a wizard's house. But Merlin

was a good wizard so he was happy to invite Jenny's mother in as well.

"This book," said Merlin, "contains enough magic to create anything you can possibly dream of. I want you to choose what you would like best of all, and I'll make it possible for you."

It was tempting to ask for lots of money, or a palace to live in, but Jenny remembered from her fairy tales that these things seldom worked out as you wanted them.

"I'd like to be a good speller," she said after careful thought. "Spelling words, that is, not making spells!"

"Oh, that's easy," said Merlin. And he opened the book, muttered a few strange words, and a puff of purple smoke whirled round the room. It looked terribly magical.

"You will be the best speller in England," said Merlin. "There won't be one word that will defeat you. But, as an extra surprise – because spelling is a bit dull, isn't it? – I've given you one magic wish as well. Use it wisely."

And, because Jenny is such a sensible girl, I'm sure she will.

FAIRY CAKES

Jiminy Goblin was passing the baker's one day when he spotted some delicious-looking cakes in the window. He trotted inside to ask what they were.

"Fairy cakes," said Mr Cookie, the baker.

Fairy cakes! They were golden, with little strands of sugar scattered all over them. Two thin slices of cake stood upright, like an open mouth, and the mouth was filled with cream. "I'll take half a dozen," said Jiminy. He couldn't wait to try them.

He was just making himself a cup of tea and his mouth was watering at the thought of the delicious cakes, when suddenly he stopped what he was doing and thought hard.

"*Fairy* cakes," he said to himself. "Does that mean they are enchanted? Does it mean I'll change into something horrible if I eat them? Perhaps I'll change into a *fairy*, perish the thought!"

In the end, Jiminy Goblin decided not to eat the cakes at all.

"I'll make my own," he said at last. "But I'll call them goblin cakes. And these will contain a special spell that will make anyone who eats them into my slave."

Jiminy Goblin was rather untidy. He thought it would be

a wonderful idea if he could have just a few slaves to work for him. One to darn his clothes, another to sweep his carpet, and maybe one more to do the cooking. He made a special batch of goblin cakes and invited three of his least favourite goblin friends round to tea.

"Do have a cake." He beamed at Stanley Scroggins.

"May I take one, too?" asked Betsy Bubble.

"Yum-yum," said Lennie Loafer, not even bothering to ask but greedily reaching out a hand.

Within minutes, Jiminy had three rather unwilling slaves running round his cottage, tidying up and cleaning. They grumbled and groaned, but however hard they tried they could not stop working. Jiminy Goblin took a deckchair into the garden and stretched out in the sun.

A short time later a young man passed the gate. He looked like a traveller because he had a stout stick and a bundle slung over his shoulder.

"Hey, Mr Goblin, could you spare a poor man a cup of tea?"

"Certainly," said Jiminy Goblin, and he went to the door to shout to one of his slaves.

"Gentleman here wants a cuppa. Give him one of my cakes while you're about it." For Jiminy thought that four slaves would be even better than three.

"A cake!" said the young man in surprise. "No one ever offers me a cake. I'm usually lucky if I get so much as a drink of water." He took a bite of the cake, stopped, and looked puzzled.

"Mm," he said. "I think I know what this is." He looked through the cottage window and smiled. "Ah, yes," he said. "I think you're trying to put me under some kind of spell, like those poor people in there."

"Me?" said Jiminy Goblin, feigning surprise. "A spell?"

"Well, if you're not, then take a bite of the cake yourself," said the young man. "A big bite."

"Righto," said Jiminy, for his spell was designed only to affect other people. He bit off a piece of cake and munched hard. To his surprise, the young man watched and then made a strange movement with his hand. He then turned towards the gate. Jiminy Goblin found himself following, even though he didn't want to.

"You are a very foolish goblin," said the young man, as he walked down the lane with Jiminy walking behind. "You are now *my* servant, for I have turned your spell back on itself. A wizard needs a servant, don't you agree?"

Poor Jiminy Goblin had to follow the wizard out of town, walking three paces behind him, attending to his every wish.

So far as I know he is still the wizard's servant. His three teatime slaves continued to work hard in his little cottage until the spell wore off. But by then it was their very own home as Jiminy never returned. They certainly didn't mind working hard to keep it spick and span for themselves.

THE HALLOWE'EN PARTY

"Now, children," said Miss Partridge, "next Tuesday is Hallowe'en. Can you tell me what that means?"

"Trick or treat," said Annie.

"Ghosts," said Martin.

"Witches and broomsticks," said Kate.

"Parties!" said Jack who had been to a party the previous year, and had dunked for apples and scared everyone with his monster mask.

"Parties is what I'm thinking of, too," said Miss Partridge. "A big Hallowe'en party with plenty of games. Everyone should dress up, and I'd like you to ask your mums or dads to prepare some fun refreshments – sausages made to look like broomsticks, oranges carved with funny faces, that sort of thing. Now, hands up everyone who can come."

Of course all the children's hands shot up – except for Lizzie Wimple, and she said she was busy.

"Too busy for a Hallowe'en party?" said Jack in astonishment.

"Hallowe'en's always a busy time at home," replied Lizzie, gathering her bag, hat, and coat, and making towards the door. She did not explain what it was that was keeping her from the school Hallowe'en party.

As soon as she got home, she told her mum all about it.

"It will be pathetic," she said. "All of them dressing up, and all the funny food and feeble games, and not a bit of real magic to be seen anywhere."

Lizzie's mother smiled broadly. "Well, we could do something about that," she said. "You could do a special act."

"But I said I wasn't going," said Lizzie. "And anyway, I want to go to the coven as usual."

"You could miss the coven for once," said Mum. "Think of the lovely surprise." Lizzie's mum wasn't one of those old-fashioned witches, full of nasty tricks and malice. She believed in using magic to entertain.

"All right," said Lizzie. "But could you bake me a special cake?"

The next day at school Lizzie told Miss Partridge that she would come to the party after all.

"Shall we call by to pick you up?" asked Annie, who lived in the same direction.

"No thanks, I'll make my own way," replied Lizzie.

The Hallowe'en party was to start at six o'clock. By a quarter past, all the children were there. Some were dressed as ghosts, some as witches, and others as skeletons and vampires and other creepy things. And what lovely food they had all brought – there was even a cake with black icing and blue stars on it, though no one knew who had added it to the feast.

"Light the lanterns, children," said Miss Partridge. They all went out into the playground, where a circle of pumpkin lanterns were set in a row on the wall. Very soon they were all lit up and the playground looked both welcoming and a little mysterious.

Then, just as the children were about to file inside for the games, there was a whirring, swishing noise in the air.

They all looked up . . .

. . . and saw Lizzie Wimple, dressed as a witch, flying across the playing fields towards them.

"Wow!" said Jack. "An automatic broomstick – I wonder how she makes it work."

"It's magic!" said Kate, who believed in fairies and ghosts and witches.

Lizzie flew round the playground once. She even did a loop-the-loop. Then down she came, and she offered a ride to the smallest child in the school.

"It's only a little broomstick," she explained.

Well, if Jack didn't believe in witches then, he certainly believed in magic after he'd eaten a slice of the mysterious black cake. He was the first to try it. It tasted of all the best things he had ever eaten. When he'd finished it, he felt a very strong desire to rush into the playground and take to the air. And he did, without the aid of broomstick or wings! Soon the whole school had tasted the wonderful cake and the air was filled with flying children and teachers!

It was a wonderful Hallowe'en party.

"Well," said Lizzie to herself, getting back on to her broomstick, "I always knew Mum baked light cakes, but she must have used masses of self-raising flour for this one!"

THE NEW BROOM

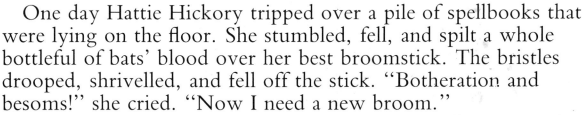

There was once an old witch called Hattie Hickory. She lived, as most witches do, in a crooked old cottage with dark rooms and cobwebs in every corner.

Shelves bulged with leather-bound books of spells, and cupboards were full of bottles and boxes of potions and pills. It was all dreadfully untidy, but then that's the way witches like it to be.

One day Hattie Hickory tripped over a pile of spellbooks that were lying on the floor. She stumbled, fell, and spilt a whole bottleful of bats' blood over her best broomstick. The bristles drooped, shrivelled, and fell off the stick. "Botheration and besoms!" she cried. "Now I need a new broom."

"What you need," said her cat, "is an assistant."

An assistant! Hattie Hickory stopped trying to spoon the bats' blood into the bottle and thought hard. "An assistant would clear away all the spellbooks," thought Hattie Hickory. "I wouldn't fall over them then. She'll be able to go into the woods and gather all the ingredients for my spells while I have a nice snooze after lunch."

"I'll advertise," said Hattie Hickory out loud.

A week later Daphne Doogood arrived. She was a neat, plump-looking lady with a brisk, no-nonsense manner. She wasn't quite the sort of person Hattie had in mind. She would have preferred a thin, starved orphan whom she could boss about, but Daphne would have to do as nobody else had applied for the position.

"Right," said Hattie Hickory. "You can start at once. I'm just off into town to buy a new broomstick. I want you to pick up all the spellbooks and put them on the shelves where they belong. Then you can arrange all the bottles and boxes in alphabetical order, so that I know what I'm looking at."

Daphne Doogood beamed. This was exactly the type of work she liked doing – tidying up.

Hattie Hickory was gone for longer than she expected. She was fussy about her broomstick. One was too short in the handle; another's bristles were too soft. She tried three shops before she found exactly what she wanted, and then she had to go over to the wizard's house for a flying spell to make her new broomstick take to the air.

When at last she landed in the garden of her cottage, she wasn't sure if she had come to the right place. The windows were flung wide open. Freshly washed curtains hung on the line, billowing in the breeze. The hedge had been cut and the herb garden weeded.

When she pushed the door open she could smell the terrible smells of disinfectant and furniture polish! A sad line of damp-looking spiders scurried past her into the garden.

She did not recognise her own living room. It was sunny and bright and there was not a cobweb in sight. The furniture gleamed with fresh polish and a vase of yellow daffodils stood on the corner of the table.

Not even Spitfire her cat had escaped. She cowered under the table, her fur brushed and a velvet collar round her neck.

Daphne Doogood was just tipping Hattie's collection of stuffed toads into the dustbin.

"WHAT ARE YOU DOING?" roared Hattie Hickory, in horror.

Daphne Doogood beamed.

"Doesn't it look so much better," she said. "You could eat a meal off your floor now. By the way, I've thrown all those horrible dusty old books on to a bonfire."

"Oh no!" shrieked Hattie Hickory, dashing out of the kitchen door and into the back garden. It was true. A bonfire was blazing merrily away, and she could see the remnants of her spellbooks crumbling into ashes.

"You!" she cried, turning to Daphne Doogood who was now busily trimming the lawn. "I'll turn you into a rat – I'll give you purple boils – I'll – "

But of course she could do none of these things. She had no spellbooks.

Spitfire was sitting on the wall, her fur dried, looking more cheerful. "Tee-hee," she tittered. "A new broom, eh? An assistant, eh? They always say there's nothing like a new broom to sweep away old and unwanted things. Well, it seems you have *two* new brooms, now!"

NAT'S MAGIC SEEDLING

There was something strange about the little seedling Nat found growing by his garden fence. It was bright blue for one thing and, for another, it seemed to shoot up about ten metres a night. By the end of the week Nat's seedling was growing like Jack's beanstalk, high above the rooftops and into the clouds!

Nat stood in his garden a few mornings later and stared up at his blue plant whose top was now out of sight. On the stem grew little nodules, like footholds. It was just waiting to be climbed and Nat, wondering what on earth was at the top of it, decided to do just that.

So up and up he climbed, right up through the damp clouds, and still the blue plant towered above him. Now and then Nat could see bright blue leaves sprouting, and then, as he emerged from a damp and grey cloud, he could see one beautiful golden flower glittering in the sunshine.

"It looks like real gold," thought Nat. "I could pick it now and return home, and my fortune would be made."

But the plant still rose above him, beckoning him on.

"I'll find a giant at the top, I bet," said Nat to himself. "Then I'll be sorry I didn't pick the golden flower."

Nat was not greedy, but he was very adventurous, so on and on he climbed till at last he saw the blue, feathery top of the plant, rising above a cloud.

Nat was not really surprised when he found that he could stand on the cloud. "I'll see a castle soon, I suppose," he thought. But as he straightened himself he saw something quite different.

It was a wizard. There was no doubt about that. The wizard was dressed in deep midnight blue. He wore a splendid cloak with golden stars on it, and a tall, conical hat.

Nat looked at the wizard and the wizard looked at Nat.

"Have you anything in your pocket?" demanded the wizard. He looked very fierce.

Nat trembled. "Not much," he said. He pulled out a dirty handkerchief, a corkscrew, and a penny whistle.

"No golden flower?" asked the wizard.

Nat remembered how he had nearly, but not quite, been tempted into picking the flower.

He shook his head.

To his surprise, the wizard slapped him hard on the back.

"Splendid fellow," he said. "D'you know, you are the only person who has ever reached the top of the plant. And do you know why? Because everyone who climbs the plant always picks the golden flower and then goes home. Much good it does them, too, for as soon as their feet reach the ground, it turns into a stinking, mouldy mess. Now at last I've met someone who isn't greedy enough to put his own personal fortune before his natural curiosity."

The wizard reached into his pocket and took out a small wooden box.

"D'you know what's in here?" he asked. "It's another seedling. Now, if you follow my instructions carefully, you'll find it only grows to the height of a sunflower, and it will flower twice a year."

Nat listened to what the wizard told him. He was never to water the plant. He was to clean its blue shiny leaves with brass polish, and he was to sing it to sleep each night with a lullaby.

Nat went home, and he did exactly what the wizard instructed. Before long a small blue shoot appeared. And by the end of the summer, Nat had picked bunch after bunch of pure golden flowers.

THE BROOMSTICK RACE

There was once an old man who sold broomsticks to witches. He wasn't very rich, and as time went on he became poorer still. This was because there were fewer and fewer witches and, as witches are known for their meanness, those that were around seldom bought new brooms.

Poor old Mr Troopuddle wondered how he could continue to make a living out of selling witches' brooms, when he suddenly came up with a very good idea.

He would run a broomstick race. He would make a splendid broom which he would give as first prize. The broomstick race would take place on Friday 13th May – a most lucky day for witches, if not for humans.

Mr Troopuddle worked away all week at his prize broom. It was very splendid. It had a polished wooden handle and a carved cat's face. Mr Troopuddle put the broomstick in the window of his shop, together with a poster advertising the race.

By the end of the week every single witch had agreed to take part. Nobody bought a new broom for the occasion, of course. Mr Troopuddle hadn't supposed that they would, but that wasn't his plan . . .

Friday 13th May was a gloomy, windy day, just right for witches. Up they all got on to their decrepit old broomsticks, their cats clinging on desperately. Some never made it beyond Nightshade Woods for the twigs on their broomsticks came apart. Some lost their way among the grey clouds. Some tried to do fancy things, like a loop-the-loop or figures of eight, but only succeeded in falling off. Three made it back to the finishing line, Mr Troopuddle's shop. Witch Hellebore was the winner.

She grabbed her broomstick prize with greedy glee.

"What a wonderful broom!" she crowed. "I'll be the smartest witch at the coven!"

"Aren't there any consolation prizes?" grumbled the two runners-up, so Mr Troopuddle took pity on them and handed them brand-new but very ordinary-looking brooms.

"I want one like hers!" wailed Witch Muckleberry.

"So do I!" shouted Witch Batswing. "Exactly like hers!"

Both witches grabbed at Witch Hellebore and her wonderful broom, but she swept out of the shop and into the sky before they could cast so much as a simple spell to blow her broom apart.

"Well, can you make a broom just like that for me?" grumbled Witch Batswing. "I suppose I shall have to pay for it."

And Witch Muckleberry, not to be outdone, ordered a new broom, too.

Mr Troopuddle's plan worked. Witches are terribly jealous and vain creatures. They hated to see Witch Hellebore and the two runners-up on bigger and better brooms than their own. Before long, every single witch who had taken part in the race had ordered a new deluxe broom. Mr Troopuddle made a fortune and retired to a dear little cottage, far away from witches and their jealous ways.

THE MAGIC BICYCLE

It looked such a perfectly ordinary sort of bicycle. Ellie had received it for her eighth birthday, and at first she had been very disappointed because she had so wanted a pony. The bicycle was black with a golden stripe, and it had a large, shiny silver bell. If you looked very carefully, just under the saddle, you would discover a little scattering of golden stars.

It was when Ellie first discovered the stars that she had the idea that her bicycle might be rather special. No one else she knew had a bike with golden stars on it.

"Where did you buy it?" she asked Mum.

"From that funny little shop just by the roundabout on the edge of town," replied Mum.

Ellie knew it. It was full of old and dusty second-hand bicycles. Hers was very smart by comparison.

"I couldn't
understand it,"
said Mum. "It was
going very cheap, and
yet it looks quite new."
"Stranger and stranger,"
thought Ellie.

Ellie couldn't wait to try out
her new bike. She decided to ride
down the hill to the village on it. She
tried the brakes before she set out, to make
sure they worked well. Then off she went.

Steeplechase Hill was quite scary. The hill
was very, very steep, and there was a sharp bend
at the bottom. As Ellie went whizzing down the hill
at top speed she began to apply her brakes, but they
didn't work! Faster and faster she went! She was just
wondering whether she could fling herself off the bike into
the ditch when she reached the bend at the bottom, when
something extraordinary happened! The bicycle gave a little
buck, just like a pony, and leapt right across the bend to where
the road straightened out again.

"Wow!" thought Ellie. "That was a close shave."

She patted her bike absent-mindedly as though it were a pony. It certainly acted like one. As Ellie rode the bike down towards the village it kept giving excited little bucks, and Ellie could swear she could hear it whinnying.

When she got home again she took a look at the little golden stars under the saddle. They were horseshoe shaped. She hadn't noticed that before.

"I bet I'm the only person in the world with a pony-bicycle," thought Ellie.

Every day Ellie would take her bicycle for a canter. Sometimes she took it across the field where it would vault the hedge. Sometimes she would ride it over the downs. She felt sure that if she treated it like a pony for long enough, one day it might become one.

Well, I did see Ellie riding along the village street on a little black pony the other day, so perhaps it did.

THE MONSTER UNDER THE PAVEMENT

Kerry saw monsters everywhere. They were in the airing cupboard, under the bed, even behind her wardrobe. Often at night she would lie awake, trembling, as she saw the shadow of a monster on the wall.

"There are no such things as monsters," said her mum one day when Kerry came running to tell her that the Airing Cupboard Monster was curled up on the spare duvet. "It's probably the cat."

But Kerry knew better.

One day Kerry was out walking with her mum when something grabbed her by the ankle.

"Mum!" screamed Kerry. "There's a monster under the pavement!"

"Don't be silly, dear," said Kerry's mum.

She was walking along the road looking at her shopping list, and she didn't notice that Kerry was standing stock-still, trying to free herself. A pair of skinny hands was poking up through a manhole, trying to drag Kerry down.

"MUM!" cried Kerry, but before she could open her mouth to scream again, she found herself falling into the manhole, until *splash!* she landed in a cold, underground stream.

Someone, or something, dragged her from the swiftly-flowing water and sat her on a narrow ledge. She opened her eyes fearfully. It was a monster all right, though rather a small one. It had three eyes, fluffy black fur, and huge pink ears. It was probably rather handsome, as monsters go.

"Why have you brought me here?" asked Kerry, when she could find her voice.

"We want our monsters back," said the black fluffy monster.

"What can I do about it?" asked Kerry. "And anyway, back from where?"

"From the airing cupboard, from under your bed, and from behind the wardrobe," replied the monster. "They're trapped, didn't you notice?"

Kerry confessed she had been so scared that she hadn't really looked properly.

"Well, back home you go, then," said the monster. "Just set them free, open the manhole cover, and down they'll come."

He took Kerry's hand, and they climbed up a long ladder to the surface again.

"Goodbye," said the monster. "Don't forget, now."

As if she could!

Mum was still standing on the pavement, trying to read if she'd written "potatoes" or "tomatoes".

"Hi, Mum," said Kerry, climbing out of the manhole and on to the pavement.

"Oh, there you are, dear," said Mum. "I thought you'd gone home again."

"Er – if you don't mind, I think I will. I have something important to do," said Kerry. She knew Mum would let her because Gran was staying.

Kerry ran back home, and knocked loudly on the front door. Gran opened it.

"I'm just getting lunch," she said. "So please don't get in my way."

"I won't," said Kerry happily, and she ran upstairs, glad that the coast was clear.

First she went to the airing cupboard.

The monster inside had burrowed into a pile of ironing and had a shirtsleeve wrapped right round his neck. Kerry carefully untangled it and the monster hopped out. It looked like the Sewer Monster's baby brother.

"Come with me," said Kerry.

Then Kerry looked under her bed. Oh dear, the Under-the-bed Monster was stuck to the floor by an old half-eaten toffee. Kerry carefully unstuck him.

Behind the wardrobe, Kerry found the third monster. Its fur was caught on a nail and Kerry snipped it free with her scissors. Kerry stood at the top of the stairs and listened. She could hear Gran opening the oven door.

"Come on, quickly," she said to the three monsters, and they followed her down the stairs, out of the door, and on to the pavement. She struggled a bit to lift the manhole cover, but at last she did so, and the monsters all jumped down into the black hole. She heard them all go *splash!* at the bottom.

"I hope they're all right," she thought, and then she saw three pairs of eyes looking up at her, and faintly, from the very bottom of the hole, there came a big cheer.

THE MAGIC STONE

It was Jason who found it lying in the gutter by the side of the lane where he and his sister Evie lived.

"It's just an old stone," said Evie, looking at the dull grey pebble in her brother's hand.

"It's an interesting shape," said Jason. "Look, it's absolutely round, like a ball."

"Throw it away," Evie told him. "You've got enough junk as it is."

But Jason put it in his pocket and forgot all about it.

That night, while he was reading under the bedclothes, Jason was suddenly aware that his bedroom looked very light. Surely his bedside lamp wouldn't shine as brightly as that? He poked his head from under the duvet. The light was coming from the left-hand pocket of his jeans!

"The stone!" he said to himself. "It must be!"

He padded across the room to his chair, and dipped his hand into the pocket.

"Ouch!" he muttered. "That hurt!" The stone was red-hot, even though the outside of his jeans seemed unaffected. He took a handkerchief, wrapped it round his hand, and pulled the stone from his pocket. Immediately the room was filled with a light so brilliant that Jason had to shade his eyes. He felt a bit scared. Surely someone would notice the light from the road. What was the stone? Had someone dropped it? Had it come from outer space?

Then, suddenly, the light faded. The stone, as bright as the sun a moment before, glowed a soft yellow, then faded to an ordinary stone-colour.

"It's very dark," thought Jason. "There's not even a moon. But that's strange, the moon was shining a moment ago." Jason remembered looking at it before he got into bed. He went to the window and pulled the curtains open. Clouds had gathered and the moon was hidden.

"Does the stone react to moonlight?" Jason wondered, and decided to speak to Evie. She was the clever one. Perhaps she could work it out.

But when Evie arrived in his room, her eyes heavy with sleep, she didn't believe what had happened.

"Are you mad or something?" she said. "I told you it's just an ordinary stone, anyone can see that. Did you wake me up just to show me your mouldy old stone?"

Jason's eyes filled with tears. It was rotten not to be believed. Then, just as Evie was going out of the door, it happened again. The moon came out from behind the clouds, and the stone started to shine so brightly that it dazzled them.

"Crikey!" said Evie, her mouth open.

"We'd better put it back where we found it," said Jason. "It's weird. It must belong to someone – or something."

"How can we put it back?" asked Evie. "We'd wake the whole neighbourhood with that bright light."

Just as the two children were standing there, deciding what to do, something quite extraordinary happened.

"Look at the moon, Evie!" cried Jason. "It's coming nearer!"

"And it does have a real face!" gasped Evie. "It looks as if it's searching for something."

Jason immediately knew what to do. He went over to his chair where he'd put the stone, wrapped his handkerchief round his hand again, and carefully put the stone on the windowsill. Then he opened the window.

The moon's face filled the window. It looked quite frightening close up. Quite how it managed to pick up the stone, the children never knew. The light was too bright now to look. But as the light gradually faded, Evie and Jason went to the window and looked out. The stone had gone and the moon was back in its usual position, but its huge round face could still be seen. And it was smiling!

CAT ON A BROOMSTICK

"One day," said Jetstone, "I shall definitely go on strike."

Jetstone was a witch's cat. He had been specially chosen by Witch Humpledink because he had no white hairs anywhere, and he had bright green eyes that shone like emeralds.

When Jetstone had first arrived at Witch Humpledink's cottage, he thought life was going to be very comfortable from that day on. There was a roaring fire with an iron cauldron bubbling and boiling over it. There was a rag rug in front of the fire where Jetstone settled comfortably, paws tucked contentedly under him. But as soon as night fell, Witch Humpledink was up and about and calling for Jetstone to get up on her broomstick.

How Jetstone hated that broomstick! How he hated riding across the wintry sky, the wind whistling past his ears, and the cold from the snow and sleet seeping into his bones. Witch Humpledink didn't seem to notice the cold. Besides, she had her thick green cloak on, and a hat. "But I can't complain," thought Jetstone. "She might change me into a mouse!"

One particularly foul evening, when the rain was lashing against the cottage windows, Jetstone decided that he had had enough. "I don't want to be a witch's cat any longer," he muttered. "I want a nice, warm farmhouse kitchen, where I can catch mice during the day and sleep all night by the warm stove."

"Come on, Jetstone," shouted Witch Humpledink. "Time to go out."

"I'm on strike," thought Jetstone, and pretended not to hear.

"JETSTONE!" roared Witch Humpledink. "Come here AT ONCE, or I'll turn you into a frog."

Jetstone heard this and slowly got to his feet, stretched, and reluctantly followed the witch to the door. The wind was blowing a gale outside and the rain blew in through the open door, soaking Jetstone's face.

Witch Humpledink grabbed hold of him and plonked him behind her on the broomstick. Jetstone dug his claws in and clung on tight as the broomstick rose in the air and wove an uneven course across the wood.

"Wonderful weather for witches!" cried Witch Humpledink, enjoying the wind and the rain.

"It's now or never," said Jetstone, looking down from the broomstick to the wood below. Witch Humpledink was enjoying herself so much that she had forgotten all about her cat sitting behind her. He balanced precariously on the shaking broomstick, and then he jumped.

It was a long way to the ground, and Jetstone was absolutely terrified as he fell down and down. But, being a cat, he landed the right way up on his four feet, on soft wet grass. Still shaking, he waited till the broomstick was out of sight. Then, soaking wet and freezing cold, but free, he ran all the way through the wood until he reached a farmyard. He dived into an open barn, shook off some of the rain, and settled down in the soft hay. His heart was still hammering with fright, but eventually he calmed down and fell fast asleep . . .

"Look, a black cat!"

"Is he a stray?"

"He looks like Witch Humpledink's cat to me."

Jetstone opened his eyes to find the farmer, his wife, and his little daughter all looking down at him.

"No, he can't be the witch's cat," said the farmer's wife. "Look, he has white whiskers, and everyone knows that Witch Humpledink's cat is jet-black all over."

White whiskers? Jetstone could hardly believe it. He squinted down at them, and saw that they were indeed snowy white.

He remembered jumping from the broomstick, and the long run through the wood, terrified that Witch Humpledink would catch him and turn him into a frog. Perhaps his whiskers had turned white with fright. But, whatever the reason, he could no longer be a witch's cat.

"Bring him in by the fire," said the farmer's wife. "He looks hungry and cold."

Jetstone settled happily by the kitchen stove, and purred contentedly while the wind and the rain lashed against the windowpanes.

DRAGON FIRE

Once, a long time ago, dragons lived in houses like you and me. In those days they didn't breathe fire, so it was perfectly safe.

Clarence, like all dragons, loved to be warm. He loved his home with its pale blue walls and cheery red rugs. He would curl up by a roaring fire and happily snooze away, feeling very contented. Dragons do tend to spend a lot of their time sleeping.

But one cold day in the middle of winter, everything changed. Clarence was feeling the cold dreadfully. He shivered and shook as he hurried down the street towards home. It was just starting to snow and a snowflake plopped on to his nose.

"Ugh!" he said. "Poor, warmth-loving dragons like me shouldn't have to put up with this. I wish I could carry my nice warm fire with me all the time, then I'd never feel cold again." The more Clarence thought about it, the better he liked the idea.

Now, down the street, in the very end cottage, there lived a wizard. He wasn't a very good wizard and his spells often went horribly wrong, but Clarence thought he could probably manage the simple spell he wanted. By this time Clarence was nearly home, but, despite the cold, he thought his idea was such a good one that he turned and flew all the way back to the wizard's cottage.

"Hm," said the wizard. "Fire is a very tricky thing, you know. I usually don't touch it, in case it gets out of hand."

But Clarence pleaded and pleaded, and at last the wizard took down a big, thick, leather-bound book and leafed through the pages.

"Ah, here we are," he said. "Creation of fire, above, round, and underneath." He read the spell carefully, prepared his spell-making pot, and then took some dark-coloured potions from his shelf.

"We don't have any tortoise's spittle," he muttered, "but I daresay this green snake's venom will do instead." And he mixed and muttered, and muttered and mixed, until a perfectly horrible-smelling brew began to steam in the big copper pot. At last it was ready.

"Open wide," said the wizard, so Clarence closed his eyes, wrinkled his nose, and opened his big mouth wide. Ugh! It tasted absolutely disgusting. Still, he felt something was working. He suddenly began to feel very hot, especially around the mouth.

"Thank you so much," he said, and he gave the wizard five pieces of his precious dragon gold.

Outside in the street, Clarence began to wonder if he'd been wrong and that he had parted with his dragon gold a little too hastily. There was no fire above, round or underneath him. The snow fell heavily and although Clarence's mouth still felt hot, the rest of him was as freezing cold as ever. If he hadn't been feeling so cold he would have gone straight back to the wizard and asked for his money back, but by now he had reached his front door and couldn't wait to get close to his fire.

As he put the key in the lock, he felt a sneeze coming on.

"Atish – atish – atishoooo! Oh help!" For as Clarence opened his mouth to sneeze, a huge flame shot out and scorched his lovely pale blue door. He sneezed again as he went into the sitting room and this time the flame caught the curtains and took hold. In less time than it takes a dragon to fly a mile, Clarence's lovely little home had completely burned down!

71

Of course, a fire-breathing dragon can't possibly live safely in a nice little house. Poor Clarence flew up into the hills to find another home that wouldn't catch fire every time he sneezed. He found a big, deep cave, and gathered some logs and branches and built a huge bonfire in front of it. He had no difficulty in lighting it. Wrapping himself in a special flame-resistant blanket, Clarence snuggled down in his cave and fell fast asleep.

Clarence was very pleased with his new home. All his dragon friends came to visit him, and they agreed it was a very dragon-like sort of place. Also, breathing fire was a jolly useful thing to be able to do.

Very soon, the not so successful wizard at the end of the lane had been visited by hundreds and hundreds of dragons. He was a big success at last!

THE LITTLE YELLOW GOBLIN

Once upon a time, under a big stone in Nightingale Lane, there lived a little yellow goblin. He was an ugly fellow, with small, mean eyes, a long, pointed nose and fingernails like curved claws. Even though he was small, he caused a great deal of trouble. If a horse went by he would leap out and scratch it on the leg. The poor animal would bolt down the road with its rider holding on for dear life!

Sometimes a crowd of children would come along, not noticing the little goblin hiding behind the stone. Occasionally a child would give the stone a kick and then the goblin would spring out, screeching loudly. He would then kick one of the children on the ankle. Even though he was such a little fellow, it hurt a lot. But the child would never see who had landed such a vicious kick.

But one day someone did notice him. He had just bitten Jane's best friend Betsy on the leg and, while Betsy hopped about, crying, Jane looked around her to see what had caused the bite. She didn't have to look far. Behind the stone she could see a small, wicked-looking, yellow face and a pair of sharp, malicious eyes.

"Hey you!" cried Jane. "Why did you just bite my friend?"

The goblin tried to hide, but Jane suddenly stooped down and grabbed him by the scruff of his neck. He spat and struggled like a wildcat, but Jane wouldn't let go.

"I asked you a question," she said.

"I know you did," snarled the goblin. "Let me go and I'll tell you."

"No fear," said Jane. "I've heard about you and if you can't be polite to me, I'll drop you in the village pond. It's very deep and very smelly, and I think you would probably drown."

The goblin started to whimper. "Oh please, no, that would be cruel. I can't swim."

"But you don't mind being cruel to other people. Why should I be kind to you? I'm sure Betsy – and all the other people you've hurt – wouldn't mind if you drowned, would you, Betsy?"

"I'd stamp on him if I were you," said Betsy, rubbing her sore leg.

"I don't see why I can't play nasty tricks," muttered the goblin, sulkily. "I'm so small that no one ever notices me. Everybody likes to be noticed sometimes."

Jane shook him hard. "You don't have to be nasty to be noticed!" she cried. "Try being nice instead."

"But it's more fun being nasty."

"Yes, it is," agreed Jane. "Right, off to the pond we go!"

"All right!" cried the goblin, struggling to escape. "I'll be nice, I promise."

"I bet he doesn't keep his promises," said Betsy.

"Goblin's word," said the goblin.

Jane let him go. "We'll know where to find you again if you don't," she threatened.

Soon after, strange things started to happen in Nightingale Lane. An old lady rested her basket by the side of the road on her way to market. When she picked it up there was a beautiful bunch of daffodils lying on the top. And a traveller spoke of a very helpful little yellow man who directed him to the nearest inn, and offered to mend the holes in his boots.

The next time that Jane and Betsy walked along Nightingale Lane they met a pleasant-faced young man, a little on the short side, with a broad grin and sparkling eyes.

"You've grown!" said Jane in amazement, looking at her old enemy, the goblin.

"Every time I do a good deed I grow a bit taller," said the goblin. "It feels very good."

"Of course it does," said Jane gently, shaking him by the hand. "But don't stop being good once you've grown as tall as you want to be."

"I won't," promised the goblin, "because I don't want to lose all my new friends."

THE MONSTER IN THE POOL

In the middle of a dark wood was a deep and murky pool. In the middle of the pool, there lived a monster. Everyone knew it was there. Some had seen its huge moon-eyes looking out at them through the water. Someone else had caught sight of a scaly claw grasping hold of a branch that overhung the pool.

Everyone knew, too, that the monster ate people. The woodcutter's great-great-great grandfather had been gobbled up whole, or so it was said. It was also said to be particularly fond of small and tender boys.

Sometimes a traveller, lost in the wood, would stumble upon it by accident. That is exactly what happened to Marcus Goodheart, on his way home from the war. Marcus was a soldier and he lived in Appleby, a pretty little village that lay to the south of the wood. Marcus was very anxious to get home. As he approached the wood, he was singing. Not far to go now!

Now, he could have skirted the wood – most people would have done so, knowing about the pool and the monster – but Marcus had been away fighting, and had seen many horrors of his own. What was a monster in a pool by comparison? Anyway, he could easily avoid it. Marcus walked briskly through the wood, still singing.

He came to a fork in the path and decided to go left, thinking Appleby lay in that direction, but he came to the pool instead. Being a brave soldier, he couldn't help stooping to look into the still and brackish water. "There's probably not a monster in there at all," he thought. "It's just a silly old fairy tale."

Then, deep, deep down in the water, something stirred and an eye glinted. Before Marcus could move away, a huge shape darted to the surface, and a wet and clammy hand grabbed his leg.

"Let me go!" cried Marcus, trying to shake off the hand, but by now the rest of the monster had emerged. It was terribly ugly, and it was a repulsive muddy-green colour.

"Let go!" cried Marcus, trying to escape.

"No – stay with me!" cried the monster.

"You can speak," said Marcus in amazement.

"Of course I can speak," snorted the monster, climbing right out of the water and up on to the bank. "Not that I get much time to practise. Nobody ever comes near me."

"Well, I'm not surprised," said Marcus, without thinking. "You're so horribly ug –"

"Ugly," said the monster, and he drooped his head. A sad tear dropped from his moon-eyes. "I'm a monster, that's why. All monsters are ugly. Otherwise they wouldn't be monsters."

Marcus realised that the monster had let go of his leg, but he didn't run away. This monster was not evil, he could see that. Only lonely and very, very sad.

"I expect you'd look very handsome to another monster," Marcus said kindly. "But people are afraid of you, you see, because you would eat them."

"Eat them!" exclaimed the monster. "Who told you that? I'm a vegetarian."

"But what about the woodcutter's great-great-great grandfather?" asked Marcus.

"You don't think I'm as old as all that, do you?" asked the monster. "That was my great-great-grandfather, the last man-eating monster in the family. All I want is a bit of company and a chat."

Marcus Goodheart reached out and took hold of the monster's clammy hand. "I'll come to see you," he promised. "Every Monday at four o'clock. And I'll bring my three children, too, so that when I go back to the war you'll still have company."

The monster's big moon-eyes glowed. When Marcus looked into them he saw the kindness there. He knew his children would be perfectly safe with the monster.

The monster still lives in the pond but now he has plenty of company. The villagers learned from Marcus that their fears were quite unfounded, and there's now a well-beaten path leading to the middle of the wood. The monster's pool has become a very popular place for picnics, and people bring him his favourite food – strawberry buns!

ALL THAT GLITTERS . . .

Barnaby Bassett had a nice little cottage, a cheerful wife who cooked well and laughed at all his jokes, and a fine black-and-white cow who gave the couple plenty of good, creamy milk.

Despite the comfort of his life, Barnaby Bassett was not happy. He longed for just one thing. He wanted his cellar to be filled with bags of gold. He didn't want to spend it, he just wanted to gloat over it. He had the makings of a true miser.

"Just one bag of gold would be sufficient," he said.

One evening Mary Bassett was sitting by the fire, reading a book, and Barnaby was fretting about the gold he didn't possess. There came a knock at the door. Barnaby went to answer it and found, standing on the doorstep, a funny-looking little man dressed in green with a red feather in his cap. He had pointed ears, a long nose, and was no taller than Barnaby's kneecap.

"I'm wondering whether you'd be good enough to sell me that fine cow I've just spotted in the byre," said the little man.

"Sell her? Why, she's all we have," replied Barnaby.

"Don't even think of it," said his wife, who didn't much like the look of the little man.

"She's a fine cow," went on Barnaby, suddenly wondering whether he could make his dream come true. "She would be worth her weight in gold."

"It's gold I'll be offering you," said the little man.

Barnaby's eyes gleamed.

The little man pulled from behind his back a large, bulging sack. From it he took a handful of gold coins that glittered in the light of Barnaby's lantern.

"Bite a coin and see if it's real," he told Barnaby.

With trembling fingers Barnaby took the coin and bit hard on it. It was certainly real.

"All right," he said quickly, before the little man changed his mind, and before his wife could say anything to stop him. "She's yours!"

"Don't bother to come out," said the little man. "I'll take her now, if you have a halter. Here's the gold."

Off he went to the byre to unfasten the Bassetts' cow. Barnaby came inside, rubbing his hands.

"Help me with this sack, Mary," he said. "It's very heavy."

"I only hope you've done the right thing," sighed Mary, getting to her feet. "I didn't like the look of that little chap. He looked like a leprechaun to me, and you know how mischievous they can be."

She came over to the door and they each took hold of a corner of the sack and pulled. To their amazement it slid easily over the floor, as though it only contained featherdown.

With a sinking heart, Barnaby undid the sack. Inside was a pile of old leaves.

"B-but it was gold, real gold, truly it was," he stammered.

"I told you not to sell the cow," said Mary crossly, "but, oh no, you wouldn't listen." The Bassetts rushed to the window and looked out. The byre was empty and there was no sign of either the little man or the cow.

"Perhaps now you'll stop dreaming of what you can't have, and work for what you can," snapped Mary.

From that time onwards Barnaby did just that. He worked and worked until he had saved up enough money for another cow. He had no time at all to think about piles of gold.

NOT QUITE A DRAGON

Rachel and Patrick found it one day while they were walking home from school. Patrick was kicking an old tin can along the pavement and Rachel told him to put it into a nearby litter bin. She was like that – very neat and a bit bossy. Patrick scowled but picked up the can, and was just about to throw it into the bin when he let out a cry.

"*Rachel!* There's something alive in there!"

The two children peered into the mess of old newspapers, hamburger boxes, and tin cans. Something was moving underneath the paper. A head popped out.

It was like nothing the children had ever seen before! It had bright, amber-coloured, bulging eyes, and a scaly skin like a lizard. It was a sort of greeny-yellow colour. It wasn't very big – about the size of a small cat – and it was trying hard to scramble out of the bin, clutching on to the pile of rubbish with long, curved claws.

"It's a dr-dragon," stuttered Patrick.

"Not quite a dragon," said Rachel, staring. "It's too small, and it has rather nice eyes."

"A bit like E.T.," remarked Patrick, regaining his courage. "D'you think we ought to help it out?"

"Of course," said Rachel, suddenly taking hold of the small creature by the middle and hauling it out of the disgusting mess of the litter bin. It clung to her, its sharp claws catching in her sweater.

"Ouch, you're *hurting* me," she said, gently unhooking the creature's claws. It cuddled down in her arms, looking up at her pleadingly with its huge amber eyes.

Patrick put out a finger and gently stroked its scaly head.

"Can we take it home with us?" he asked. "Oh, do let's."

Rachel sighed. They had just lost their old dog and she knew Patrick missed having a pet. But this? What would it eat? And what would Mum say?

"It would really be best to put it on the pavement," she said. "It may make its own way home – wherever that is."

She put the small creature down and both children hurried off down the street. Patrick stopped and looked back. The little thing was trying to keep up with them in a series of small hops and jumps. Then it unfolded a pair of tiny wings and fluttered along behind them.

"Oh dear," said Rachel. "I don't know what Mum –"

But before she could say any more, there was a loud whirring noise overhead. They looked up to see a huge winged beast bearing down on them. Patrick screamed and ducked, but Rachel just stood and stared. It was like the little creature, only much, much larger. It had the same marvellous luminous eyes.

One moment it was overhead, and the next it had scooped up the tiny little creature hopping along the pavement.

"Stop it!" cried Patrick. "It will kill it!"

"No, it won't, stupid," said Rachel. "Can't you see – it's the little one's mother!"

Both children stood in wonder, staring up at the sky. The winged dragon, or whatever it was, grew smaller and smaller until it was a spot in the far distance. Then it vanished. It was as though nothing extraordinary had happened at all.

"Cheer up," said Rachel, looking down at her small brother who was trying not to cry. "If we hadn't pulled it out of that bin the mother would never have seen it. It might have starved to death."

"But I wanted it as a pet," said Patrick.

"We wouldn't have known what to feed it on," Rachel said sensibly. "It was best it went back to its mother." Patrick tried to smile. He knew his sister was right. And perhaps Mum would let them have another dog. A yellowy dog with huge, amber eyes would be nice, he thought. Looking a bit like E.T.

WITCH TWINKLETOES

One day as Witch Batswing was pulling on her long black boots she noticed a large hole in the sole of one of them. "Tut, tut, this won't do," said the witch, and she took out her black purse and peered inside. "Just enough money for a pair of new boots," she declared, and off she flew to Witch Hollow to buy them.

Witch Batswing alighted from her broomstick and peered into the shoe-shop window. There were lots of boots there – fine green leather boots, shiny red boots, and ordinary black boots like her own. But the ones that took her fancy were silver and gold with diamonds sparkling all over them. Witch Batswing stared and stared, drumming her broomstick on the pavement.

They would brighten up her black clothes no end.

The other witches would hate them, of course. The Chief Witch liked conformity.

They were dreadfully expensive. Witch Batswing hadn't nearly enough money in her purse for them. But a simple magic spell should settle that.

Witch Batswing made up her mind and swept into the shop.

The boots fitted perfectly, which was strange because she had enormous feet with huge bunions on them. But as soon as she pulled them on, her feet looked slim and elegant.

"I'll take them," she said, handing the shop-assistant three gold pieces and telling him to keep the change.

"Oh, thank you, madam," said the assistant, bowing. The boots had only cost two gold coins. He was not so happy, though, when Witch Batswing had left the shop and the gold pieces turned into tin lids.

High above the trees in the black sky people thought they saw a meteor. It was dancing about in a very strange way and looked remarkably like a pair of boots. It swept off towards Spelltop Beacon, where the local witches held their coven.

"Well, what do you think of them?" said Witch Batswing to her fellow witches as she showed off her new boots.

"Vulgar," said Witch Hemlock, who had gone quite green with envy.

"TAKE THEM OFF!" roared the Chief Witch. "No self-respecting witch would ever wear boots like those! They are *far* too beautiful and elegant."

"But I'm a beautiful and
elegant witch," said Witch
Batswing, and suddenly it
was true! She was as lovely
as a princess, with fine
golden hair, and although
she still wore her black
cloak and hat, her boots
glittered and twinkled like
a million stars and her
beauty shone out like
the sun.

She was immediately banished from the coven, of course. No
witch was expected to look beautiful. She became known as Witch
Twinkletoes, and she made herb teas and potions to cure people
of spots and warts.

She never took off her magic boots. How could she? But what
will happen when she wears a hole in them, I don't know. Let's
hope there's another pair exactly the same in that little shoe-shop
in Witch Hollow!

THE WITCH AT THE BOTTOM OF THE LANE

Katie remembered meeting the witch at the bottom of the lane when she had been only three years old. She had stopped at the gate of a cottage to stroke a black cat and the witch had peered over the hedge at her. She was horrible. She had long, straggling, grey hair, and a set of yellowed and sharp-looking teeth. Her eyes burned like live coals. She opened her mouth and Katie just knew the old woman was going to seize her in her teeth, and probably eat her! Just at that moment Mum, who was walking down the lane with Katie, came along and the witch went back up the path and closed the door.

The years went by and Katie grew up. When she was four, five and six, she never went past the witch's cottage without running. When she was seven, though, she was brave enough to peep over the hedge, though not brave enough to stroke the black cat sitting on the gate-post. She had told all her friends about the witch. She had told them how, when she was only three years old, the witch had nearly eaten her.

"She had a black cloak and a tall hat and a broomstick and all," said Katie, and her friends believed her.

"She nearly cast a spell on me," said Katie. "She wanted to turn me into a frog."

One day, Mum and Katie were out shopping.

"Just pop into the baker's, love," said Mum. "We can have some special chocolate buns for tea."

Katie stood waiting her turn in the queue. The baker always sold the most scrumptious cakes. At last there was only one person in front of her. It was an old lady.

"What can I do for you, Mrs Throgmorton?" asked the baker.

"One small brown loaf," said the old lady.

"I can't tempt you into buying a chocolate bun?" joked the baker.

"I can't afford it," said the old woman, shaking her head sadly.

Katie felt dreadful as she bought her bag of chocolate buns. Fancy not being able to afford one bun! She ran out of the shop and told her mother all about it.

"That's awful," said Mum. "I know, go back inside and buy a couple more – one for the old lady's tea, and one for her to eat tomorrow."

By the time Katie had bought the buns, the old lady was nearly out of sight.

Mum and Katie hurried along after her. They shouted, but she seemed to be deaf. And then, just as they were catching her up, she turned down into the witch's lane!

Katie stopped. "Must we go down there?" she pleaded. "I don't want to go past the witch's house."

"Don't be silly," said Mum. "You're far too old to believe in witches."

Katie held tightly on to her mother's hand. She was nearly eight, but she remembered how awful it had been all those years ago, when the witch had peered at her over the hedge.

"Mrs Throgmorton!" called Katie's mum, and the old lady turned her head.

By now they had reached the witch's cottage and, to Katie's surprise, the old lady opened the gate.

"That's the witch's house!" cried Katie, pulling back. "Don't go in there!"

"It's where I live," said Mrs Throgmorton. "Always have, and always will."

Mum gave her the buns and the old lady smiled with pleasure. She did have yellow teeth, and her eyes were very bright. She was even wearing a dark cloak. But her face was kind and her smile was warm.

"When you are three years old, and someone gives you a fright, you can imagine the most dreadful things," thought Katie. "She's not a witch at all, even if she does have a black cat. She's a lonely old lady, and I expect she'd like me to visit her."

And Katie did visit, every Monday after school, with a bag of special chocolate buns.